Dear Parent:
Your child's love of reading starts here!

Every child learns to read in a different way and at his or her own speed. Some go back and forth between reading levels and read favorite books again and again. Others read through each level in order. You can help your young reader improve and become more confident by encouraging his or her own interests and abilities. From books your child reads with you to the first books he or she reads alone, there are I Can Read Books for every stage of reading:

SHARED READING
Basic language, word repetition, and whimsical illustrations, ideal for sharing with your emergent reader

BEGINNING READING
Short sentences, familiar words, and simple concepts for children eager to read on their own

READING WITH HELP
Engaging stories, longer sentences, and language play for developing readers

READING ALONE
Complex plots, challenging vocabulary, and high-interest topics for the independent reader

ADVANCED READING
Short paragraphs, chapters, and exciting themes for the perfect bridge to chapter books

I Can Read Books have introduced children to the joy of reading since 1957. Featuring award-winning authors and illustrators and a fabulous cast of beloved characters, I Can Read Books set the standard for beginning readers.

A lifetime of discovery begins with the magical words **"I Can Read!"**

Visit www.icanread.com for information on enriching your child's reading experience.

I Can Read® is a trademark of HarperCollins Publishers.

Batman: Who Is Clayface?
Copyright © 2013 DC Comics.
BATMAN and all related characters and elements are trademarks of DC Comics.
(s13)

HARP26846
Printed in the United States of America. No part of this book may be used or reproduced in any manner whatsoever without
written permission except in the case of brief quotations embodied in critical articles and reviews. For information address
HarperCollins Children's Books, a division of HarperCollins Publishers, 10 East 53rd Street, New York, NY 10022.
www.icanread.com

Library of Congress catalog card number: 2012941007
ISBN 978-0-06-188525-9
Book design by John Sazaklis

14 15 16 17 18   LP/WOR   10 9 8 7 6 5 4 3   ❖   First Edition

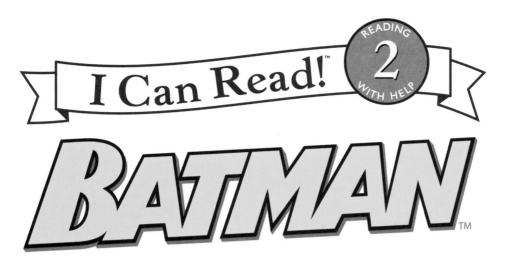

Who Is Clayface?

by Donald Lemke

pictures by Steven E. Gordon

colors by Eric A. Gordon

BATMAN created by Bob Kane

HARPER

An Imprint of HarperCollinsPublishers

BRUCE WAYNE

Bruce is a rich businessman. Orphaned as a child, he trained his body and mind to become Batman, the Caped Crusader.

MATT HAGEN

Matt was a daring treasure hunter. He discovered a mysterious pool of toxic goo, which turned him into the super-villain Clayface.

COMMISSIONER JAMES GORDON

James Gordon is the Gotham City Police Commissioner. He works with Batman to stop crime in the city.

BATMAN

Batman is an expert martial artist, crime fighter, and inventor. He is known as the World's Greatest Detective.

CLAYFACE

Clayface is a shape-shifting villain. His claylike body can mold into any shape or size.

ALFRED PENNYWORTH

Alfred is Bruce Wayne's loyal butler. He knows Bruce is secretly Batman and helps his crime-fighting efforts.

On a stormy afternoon, a man
stepped inside the Gotham City Bank.
He walked toward the front desk,
leaving muddy footprints behind him.

"Welcome, sir," greeted a teller.

"How may I help you today?"

The man smiled.

"I'd like to withdraw some money,"

he said. "One million dollars . . . cash."

The teller counted the man's money
and placed it in a large bag.

Then she handed him some papers.

"Just sign these," the teller said.

The man's hands shook with anger,
and his eyes burned red.

"Don't you know who I am?"
he asked.

Suddenly, his skin started bubbling
and bulging through his suit.

"I'm Bruce Wayne!" the man roared,
fleeing with the bag of cash.

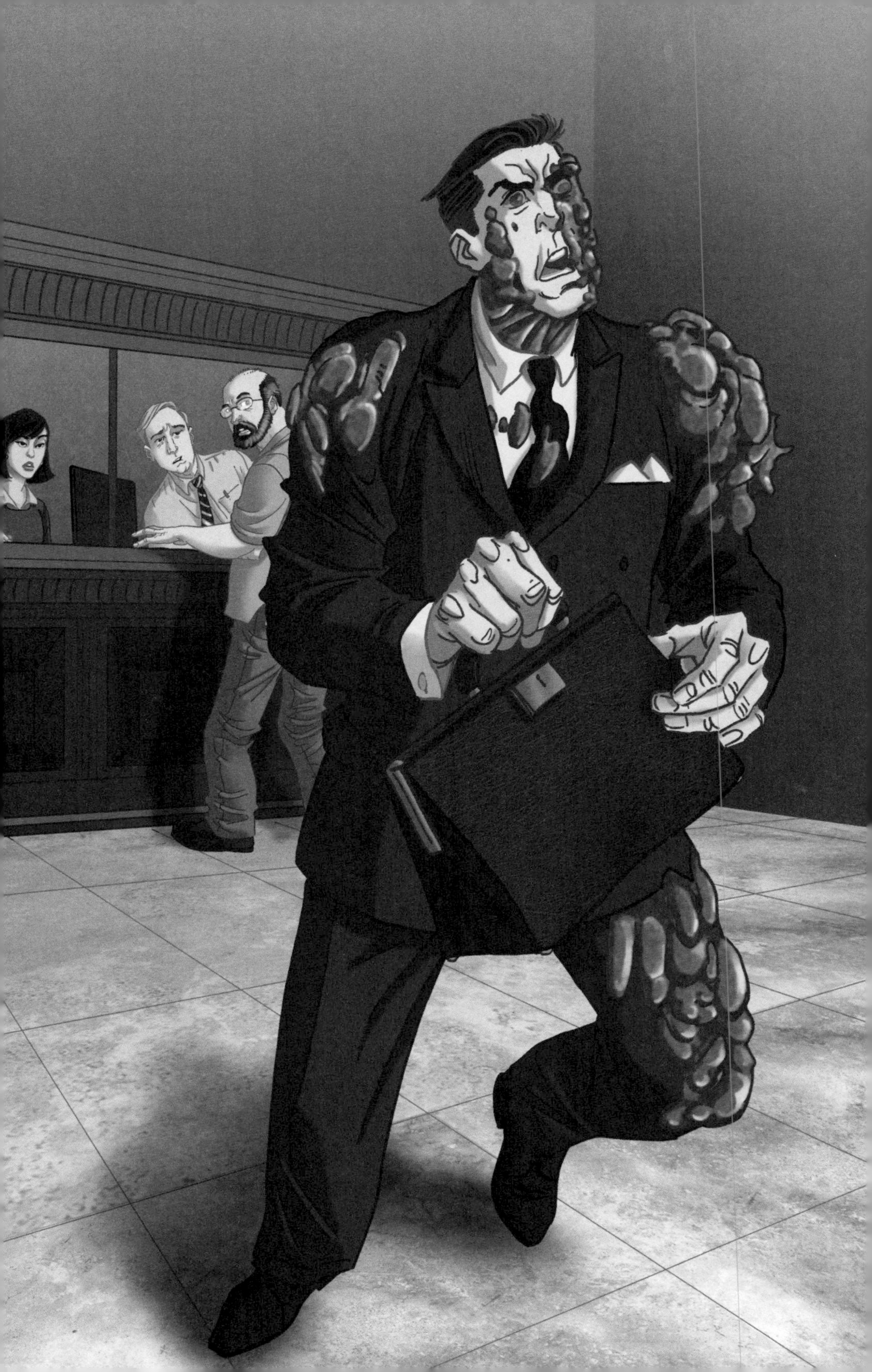

Meanwhile, Batman sped through downtown Gotham in the Batmobile.

The Caped Crusader received a
phone call from his loyal butler.
"Someone's causing a stir
at the bank, sir," said Alfred.
"Who?" asked the masked super hero.
The butler paused for a moment.
"You, Master Wayne," said Alfred,
knowing Batman's secret identity.

Moments later, the Batmobile
arrived at the Gotham City Bank.
The Dark Knight rushed inside,
but the thief was gone.

Then Batman spotted the
muddy footprints on the floor.
"This crime can be only one
man's dirty work," said the
World's Greatest Detective.

Batman followed the muddy

footprints back outside the bank.

People crowded the rainy streets,

but the trail led to only one of them.

Batman didn't know the man's face.
However, the Dark Knight knew
he'd found his criminal.
"Clayface!" the super hero shouted
at the evil mud man.

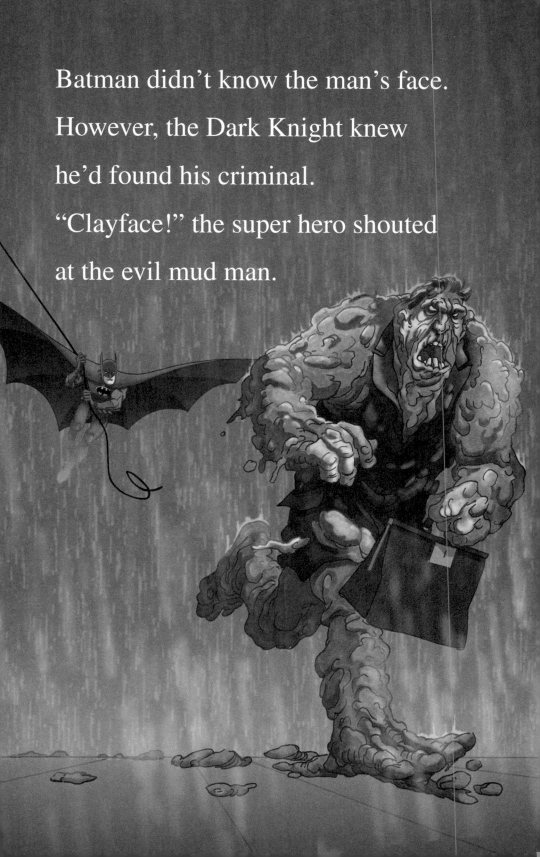

Years earlier, Matt Hagen had been
a young, daring treasure hunter.
While exploring an unknown cave,
he discovered a mysterious pool
filled with radioactive goo.
The toxic jelly changed him
into a powerful shape-shifter.
To maintain this form, Hagen
soon perfected his own toxic goo
and became the villain Clayface!

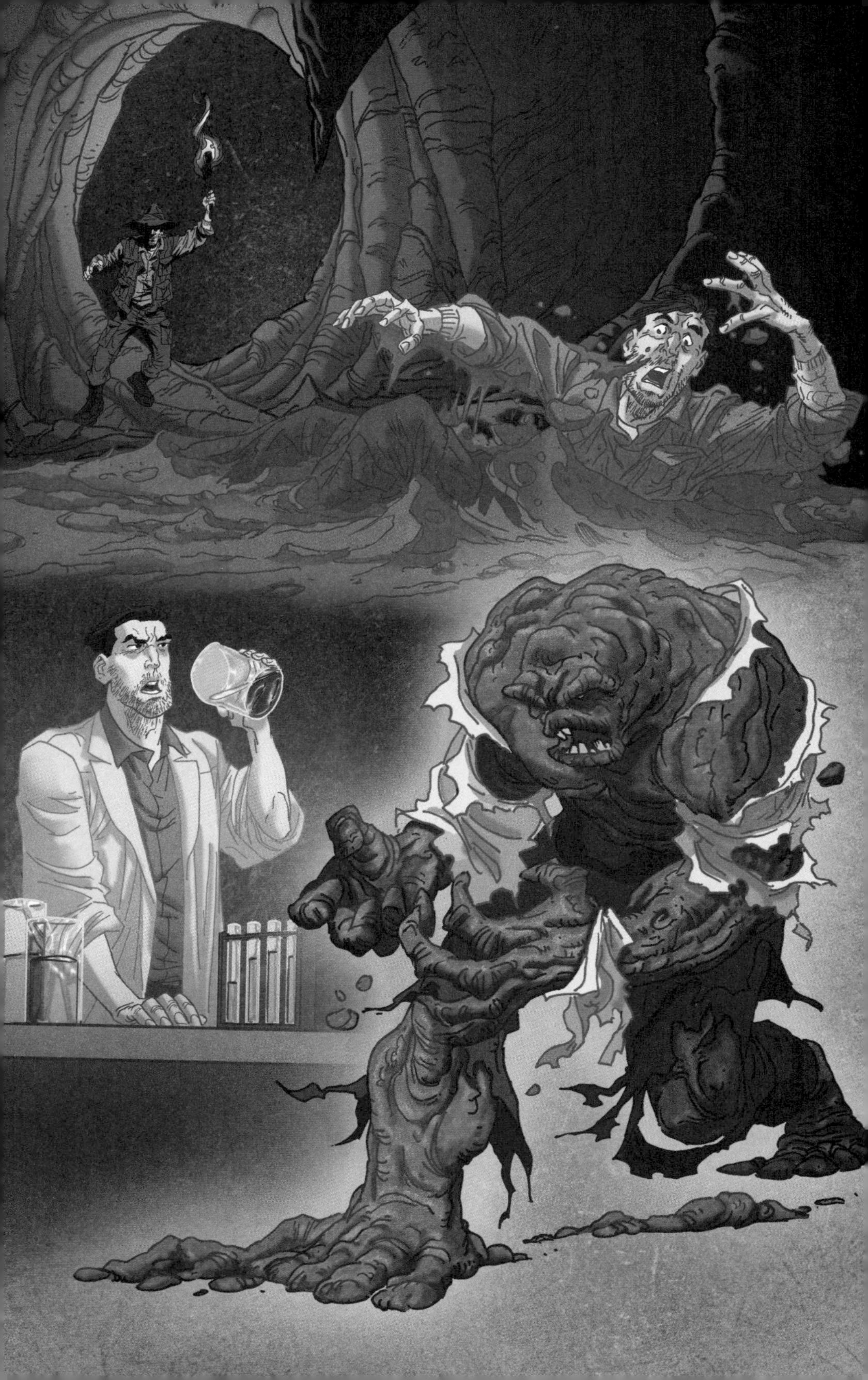

Clayface fled into the crowd.

"I'll need a bat's-eye view to

catch this crook," said Batman.

The Caped Crusader grabbed a

grapnel gun from his Utility Belt.

He fired the gun's metal hook

at a nearby building.

A super-strong wire

attached to the hook pulled the

hero high above Gotham City.

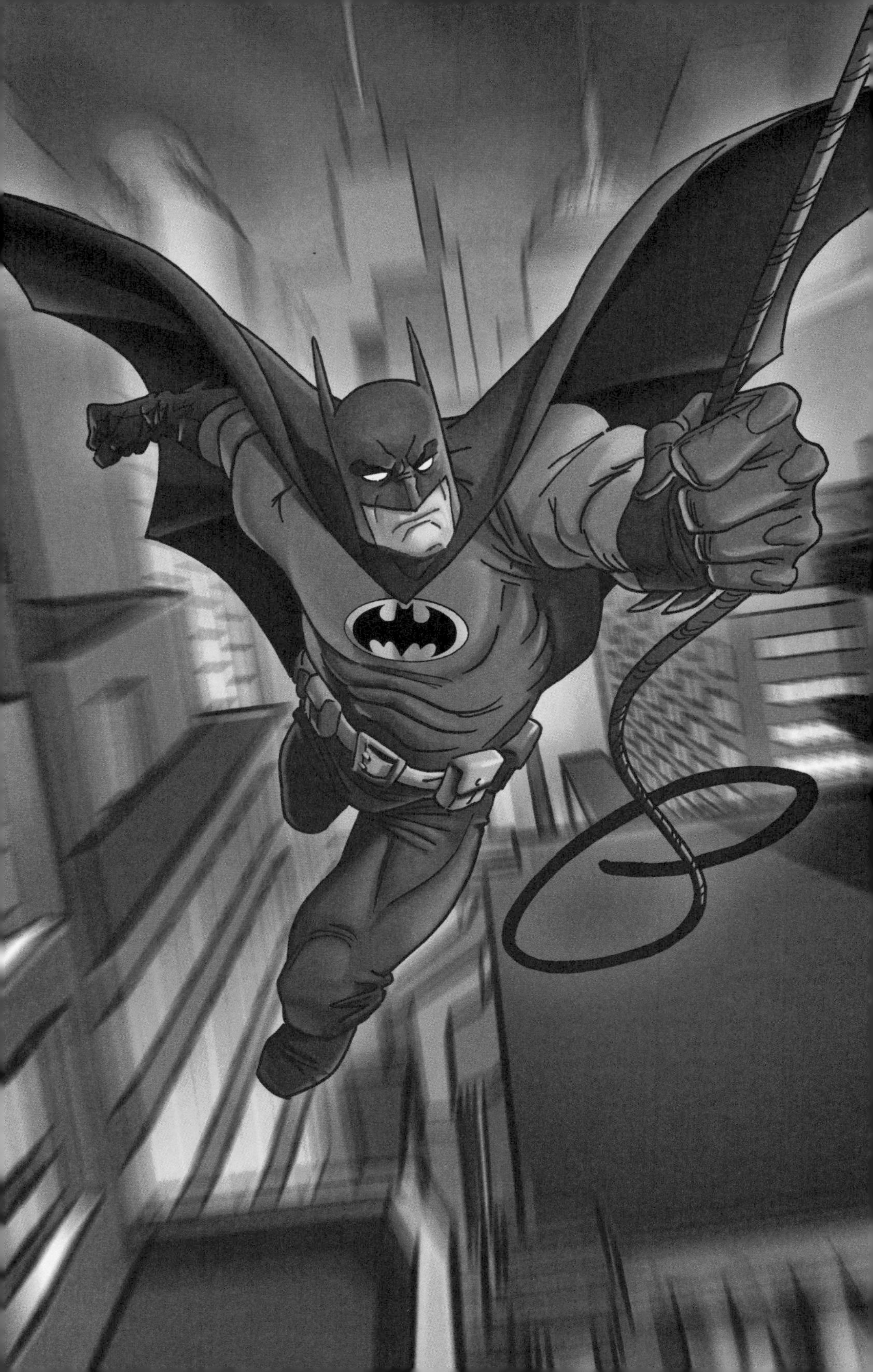

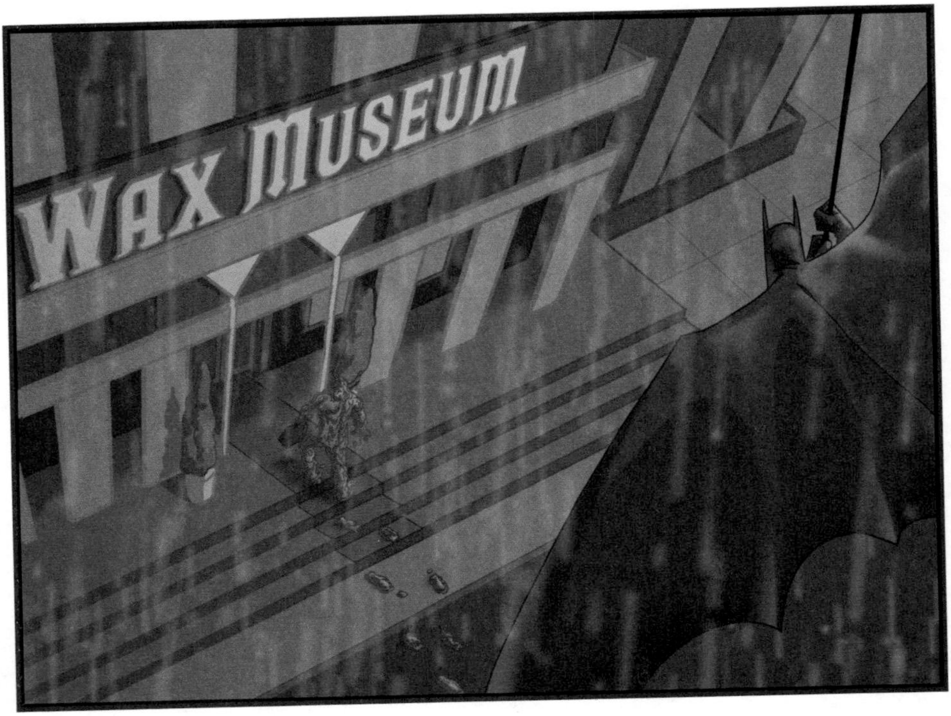
WAX MUSEUM

Soon, Clayface's soft body
weakened in the pouring rain.
Soaring over the city streets,
Batman followed his muddy trail
to shelter in the Gotham Wax Museum.
Dozens of lifelike statues
filled the rundown building.

"Clayface could be any one of these," thought Batman.

"BWAHAHA!" An evil laugh echoed through the exhibit.

Suddenly, the statue of a Spartan soldier lifted his giant spear. The villain hurled the weapon at Batman with all his might.

The Caped Crusader expertly
dodged the spear and then grabbed
a Batarang from his Utility Belt.
"What goes around, comes around,"
he said, tossing the device.

Clayface quickly changed again.
This time, he molded himself into
the Viking warrior Erik the Red!
The mud man blocked the
Batarang with a wooden shield.

The Viking villain laughed.

"You're no match for this blast

from the past," shouted Clayface.

"And soon you'll be history, too!"

"Now, prepare to walk the plank!" said the mud man, changing into the evil pirate Blackbeard. "Arrr!" The villain lunged at Batman with a sharp sword.

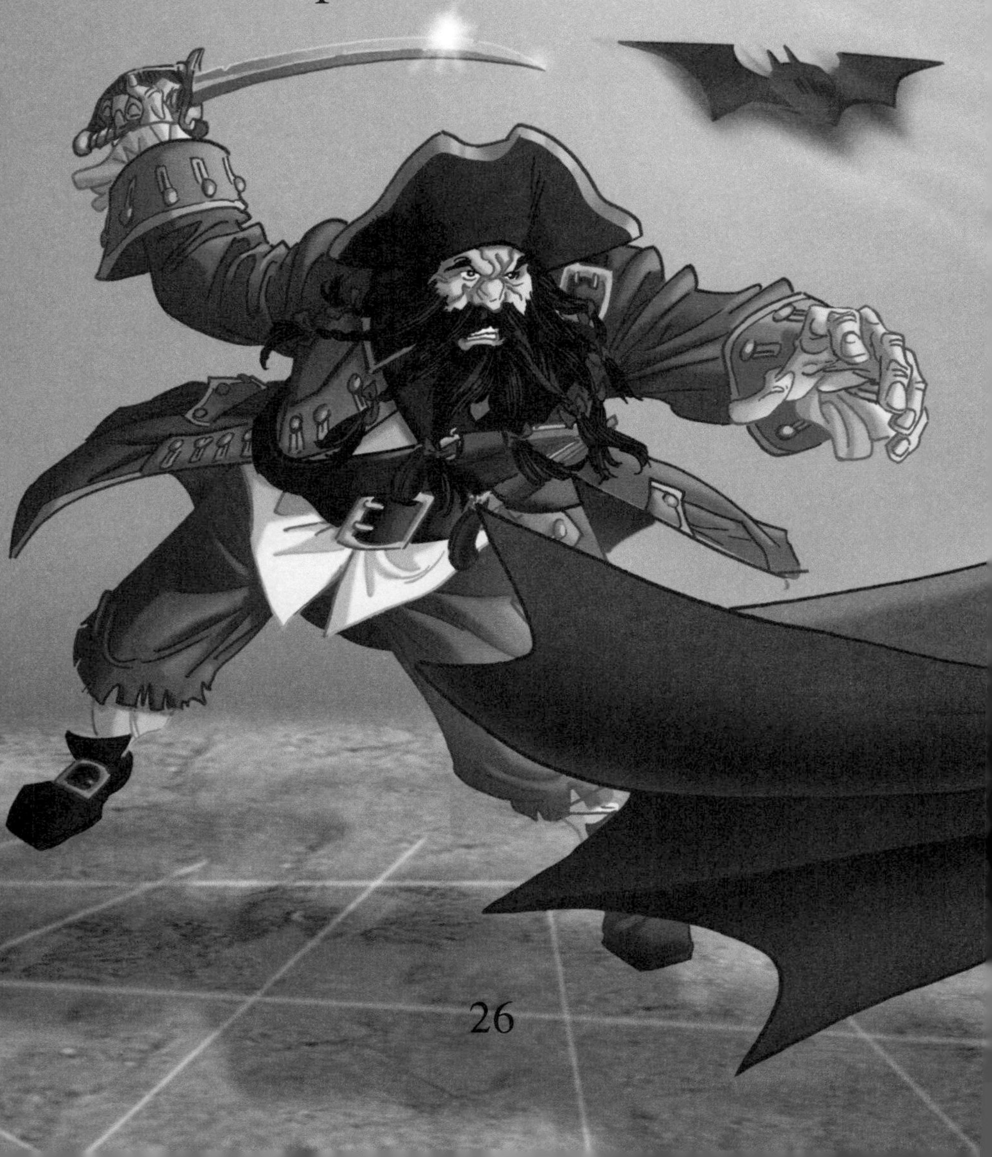

The hero flung another Batarang.
The small, winged device zipped
past the villain's hulking head.
"Missed again!" yelled Clayface.
"But you're getting warmer!"
"That makes two of us," said Batman.

At that moment, the Batarang exploded.

Wooden beams fell around Clayface

and burned like a campfire.

The villain's claylike body quickly

baked into a thick, stony shell.

The Caped Crusader knocked
on Clayface with his gloved fist.
"Looks like you'll be doing some
hard time," said the super hero,
"in Arkham Asylum."

A short while later, the police
arrived at the Gotham Wax Museum.
"That's him," said Batman, pointing
to the exhibit's newest statue.
"Good luck getting him to confess."

Police Commissioner James Gordon
shook Batman's hand.
"Don't worry," he told the hero.
"We'll get this crook to crack."

Batman took to the skies again.

"Now to clean up this money mess
at the bank," said the Dark Knight.

"I don't want the good name of
Bruce Wayne dragged through the mud."